MRER
/08

A Note to Parents and Caregivers:

Read-it! Readers are for children who are just starting on the amazing road to reading. These beautiful books support both the acquisition of reading skills and the love of books.

 The PURPLE LEVEL presents basic topics and objects using high frequency words and simple language patterns.

 The RED LEVEL presents familiar topics using common words and repeating sentence patterns.

 The BLUE LEVEL presents new ideas using a larger vocabulary and varied sentence structure.

 The YELLOW LEVEL presents more challenging ideas, a broad vocabulary, and wide variety in sentence structure.

 The GREEN LEVEL presents more complex ideas, an extended vocabulary range, and expanded language structures.

 The ORANGE LEVEL presents a wide range of ideas and concepts using challenging vocabulary and complex language structures.

When sharing a book with your child, read in short stretches, pausing often to talk about the pictures. Have your child turn the pages and point to the pictures and familiar words. And be sure to reread favorite stories or parts of stories.

There is no right or wrong way to share books with children. Find time to read with your child, and pass on the legacy of literacy.

Adria F. Klein, Ph.D.
Professor Emeritus
California State University
San Bernardino, California

Editor: Jill Kalz
Designer: Tracy Kaehler
Page Production: Lori Bye
Creative Director: Keith Griffin
Editorial Director: Carol Jones
The illustrations in this book were created digitally.

Picture Window Books
5115 Excelsior Boulevard
Suite 232
Minneapolis, MN 55416
877-845-8392
www.picturewindowbooks.com

Printed in the United States of America.

Library of Congress Cataloging-in-Publication Data
Shaskan, Trisha Speed.
The treasure map / by Trisha Speed Shaskan ; illustrated by Amy Bailey Muehlenhardt.
p. cm. — (Read-it! readers)
Summary: When George finds a treasure map next to his bed one special morning, he
follows it through his neighborhood finding a surprise at each spot marked X.
ISBN-13: 978-1-4048-2416-4 (hardcover)
ISBN-10: 1-4048-2416-2 (hardcover)
[1. Treasure hunt (Game)—Fiction. 2. Birthdays—Fiction.] I. Muehlenhardt, Amy
Bailey, 1974– ill. II. Title. III. Series.
PZ7.S53242Tre 2006
[E]—dc22   2006003408

The
Treasure Map

by Trisha Speed Shaskan
illustrated by Amy Bailey Muehlenhardt

Special thanks to our advisers for their expertise:

Adria F. Klein, Ph.D.
Professor Emeritus, California State University
San Bernardino, California

Susan Kesselring, M.A.
Literacy Educator
Rosemount–Apple Valley–Eagan (Minnesota) School District

PICTURE WINDOW BOOKS
Minneapolis, Minnesota

One morning, George found a
treasure map next to his bed.
He got dressed and started to
hunt for the hidden treasure.

The first X on the map was one block north of his house.

Treasure Map

George walked one block north to the bus stop.

There was an X on the bench at the bus stop. There was a red-and-white striped shirt lying on the bench. George put on the shirt.

8

The second X was one block east of the bus stop.

Treasure Map

George walked one block east to the park.

There was an X in the sand under the blue slide. There was an eye patch in the sand.

George shook off
the sand and put the
patch over his eye.

13

The third X was one block south of the park.

Treasure Map

George walked one block south to
Mrs. Smith's garden.

There was an X on the garden gate. There was a black pirate's hat on top of a pumpkin. George put the hat on his head.

The fourth X was one block west of Mrs. Smith's garden.

Treasure Map

George walked one block west and returned home.

There was an X on the door of his house. George opened the door.

21

Here was the hidden treasure!

"Happy birthday, George!" his friends and family yelled.

More *Read-it!* Readers

Bright pictures and fun stories help you practice your reading skills. Look for more books at your level.

Bears on Ice 1-4048-1577-5
The Bossy Rooster 1-4048-0051-4
The Camping Scare 1-4048-2405-7
Dust Bunnies 1-4048-1168-0
Emily's Pictures 1-4048-2409-X
Flying with Oliver 1-4048-1583-X
Frog Pajama Party 1-4048-1170-2
Galen's Camera 1-4048-1610-0
Jack's Party 1-4048-0060-3
Last in Line 1-4048-2415-4
The Lifeguard 1-4048-1584-8
Mike's Night-light 1-4048-1726-3
Nate the Dinosaur 1-4048-1728-X
One Up for Brad 1-4048-2418-9
The Playground Snake 1-4048-0556-7
Recycled! 1-4048-0068-9
Robin's New Glasses 1-4048-1587-2
The Sassy Monkey 1-4048-0058-1
Tuckerbean 1-4048-1591-0
What's Bugging Pamela? 1-4048-1189-3

Looking for a specific title or level? A complete list of *Read-it!* Readers is available on our Web site:
www.picturewindowbooks.com